I0893713

Just before home time, Miss Beech gives
all the children a letter.
“This letter is about our outing,”
she explains.
The children rush out with the letters.
“We are going on an outing!” they shout.

On the morning of the outing, the children arrive at school in boots and raincoats. They are all carrying lunchboxes. Miss Beech and the helpers hurry all the children onto the bus. Miss Beech has a bucket and a box of equipment.

Anna, Bill, and Seth sit at the back of the bus. They wave to the cars as they drive along.

When they arrive, Miss Beech, the helpers, and the children get off the bus and someone comes to greet them. She tells them her name is Roz.

Then she tells them to come down to the study barn, where they dump all the bags, lunchboxes, and raincoats. Next, Roz tells them what they are going to do.

The children split up, and Bill, Seth, and Anna go with Roz to the pond. They are going to do pond dipping. They have some nets and some flat plastic boxes.

They stand on a wooden platform and dip the nets into the pond. They sweep the nets about in the pond and then they empty the contents into the boxes.

They catch caddis flies and lots of tadpoles. Some of the bigger tadpoles have got legs. They catch a lot of pond weed too!

Suddenly, Anna's net slips out of her wet hands. It floats on top of the pond.

"Help!" shouts Anna. "I have lost my net." Roz takes Bill's net and hooks up Anna's one with it. The children all clap as she gives it back.
"Thank you," Anna smiles.

Meg, Gus, and Hinda go pond dipping with Roz. Anna, Bill, and Seth go with a man called Mark, who takes them on a forest trail.

They go around the trail looking for markers with different animals on. Then the children do a quiz about the animals and where they live.

Next all the children meet up again for lunch. They go down to the bottom of some cliffs, where they sit down on the sand and have a picnic.

When everyone has finished, Roz sends the children off to look for interesting things.

"Keep a look out for lucky stones, like this one," she tells them, and out of her pocket she takes a stone with a hole in it.

When the children get back, Roz is waiting for them. She has sticky-backed plastic and three boxes with different sorts of sand inside.

The children make sand hand-prints by cutting out hand shapes from the sticky-backed plastic and scattering the different sands onto them to make patterns.

The children stick the hand-prints onto card and cut them out. Roz gives out sticks and bits of string, and tells everyone to use the string to tie the hand-prints onto the sticks.

Next they tie all the interesting things they found onto the sticks as well, to make wall hangings. Roz explains that when the hangings are finished, the children can take them home.

The children look at what they have found and start to make the hangings. They cut, tie, and knot. When they have finished, they look at the hangings with Roz and Miss Beech.

Meg's stick has a big feather, a green stone, and some shells. Bill's has a twisted bit of driftwood and a float from a fishing net.

"These are very good," Roz tells them.

Hinda's stick has lots of shells and a bit of rope. Anna is very proud of her hanging. She has found some driftwood that she thinks looks like a boat, and under her sand hand-print she has tied a lucky stone!